# Happy M

D0020070

This story is filled with lots of short -a words, which appear in bold type. Here are some to sound out with your child.

| | | |
|---|---|---|
| add | castle | mad |
| and | glad | magic |
| attic | happy | rags |
| bad | has | sad |
| can | have | sash |

Cinderella **and** her
sisters **have** mail.

DISNEY
LEARNING

# PHONICS
# COLLECTION
## Short Vowels

Scholastic Inc.

Copyright © 2021 Disney Enterprises, Inc. All rights reserved. The movie THE PRINCESS AND THE FROG Copyright © 2009 Disney, story inspired in part by the book THE FROG PRINCESS by E. D. Baker Copyright © 2002, published by Bloomsbury Publishing, Inc.

All rights reserved. Published by Scholastic Inc., *Publishers since 1920.* SCHOLASTIC and associated logos are trademarks and/or registered trademarks of Scholastic Inc.

The publisher does not have any control over and does not assume any responsibility for author or third-party websites or their content.

No part of this publication may be reproduced, stored in a retrieval system, or transmitted in any form or by any means, electronic, mechanical, photocopying, recording, or otherwise, without written permission of the publisher. For information regarding permission, write to Scholastic Inc., Attention: Permissions Department, 557 Broadway, New York, NY 10012.

This book is a work of fiction. Names, characters, places, and incidents are either the product of the author's imagination or are used fictitiously, and any resemblance to actual persons, living or dead, business establishments, events, or locales is entirely coincidental.

ISBN 978-1-338-74689-1

10 9 8 7 6 5 4 3                    22 23 24 25

Printed in the U.S.A.    40

First printing 2021

Book design by Two Red Shoes Design

It is an invitation to go
to the **castle**.

Cinderella wears **rags**.

But she **has** a dress
in the **attic**.

The mice are **glad** to help.

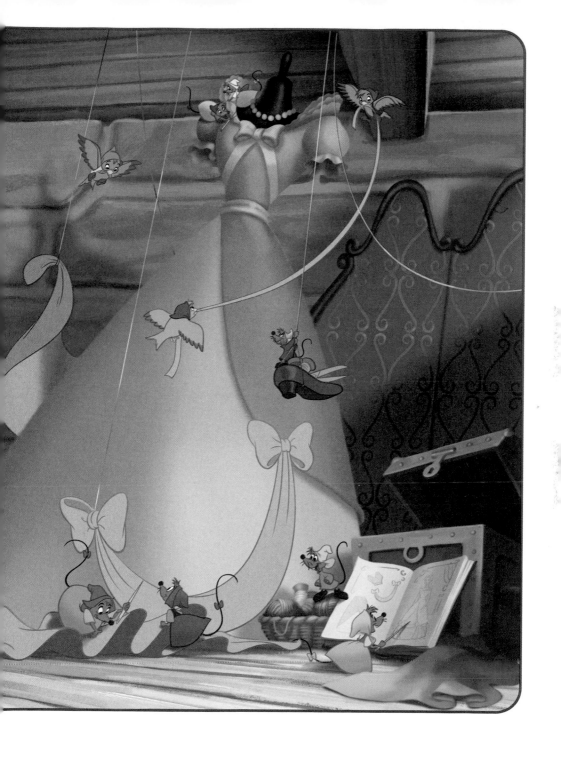

They **add** a **sash**.

It doesn't look **bad**!

Cinderella is **happy**.

Cinderella's sisters
are **mad**.

They rip the **sash**.

Now the dress looks **bad**.

Cinderella is **sad**.

Cinderella **has** a
fairy godmother!

She **has magic**.

Cinderella is **happy**.
She **can** go to the **castle**.

# A Special Guest

This story is filled with lots of short -e words, which appear in bold type. Here are some to sound out with your child.

| | | |
|---|---|---|
| friends | rescued | tended |
| guest | set | went |
| met | spell | |

Belle **set** out to find her father.

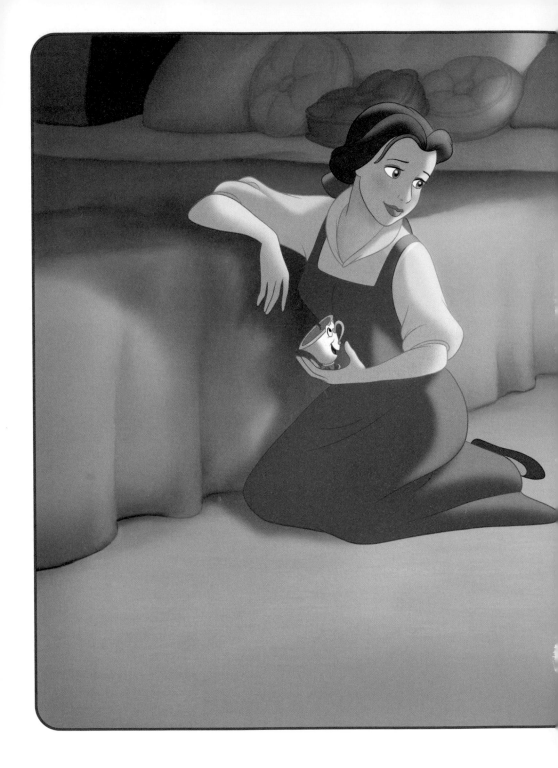

Belle **met** new **friends**.

They were under a **spell**.

Belle was their **guest**.

Belle **met** a Beast.

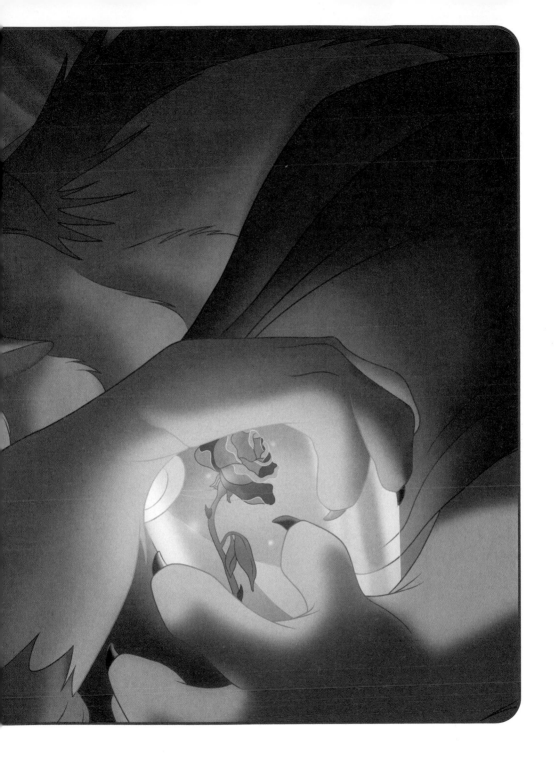

He was under a **spell**, too.

Belle **went** away.

The Beast **rescued** Belle.

Belle **tended** the Beast's cut.

They were becoming **friends**.

# The Big Ship

Book 3
short -i

This story is filled with lots of short -i words, which appear in bold type. Here are some to sound out with your child.

| | | |
|---|---|---|
| into | lit | swims |
| is | prince | tips |
| it | ship | |

Ariel **swims** to an old **ship**.

Flounder follows Ariel
**into** the **ship**.

Ariel's father does not like **it**.

Ariel **swims** to a new **ship**.

**It is lit** up.

Ariel sees a **prince**
on the **ship**.

The **ship tips**.

The **prince** falls.

Ariel **swims** with the **prince**.

They make **it**!
Ariel saves the **prince**.

# Frog Hop

This story is filled with lots of short -o words, which appear in bold type. Here are some to sound out with your child.

| | | |
|---|---|---|
| along | frogs | not |
| dog | got | on |
| frog | lost | shot |

Tiana met a **frog**
named Naveen.

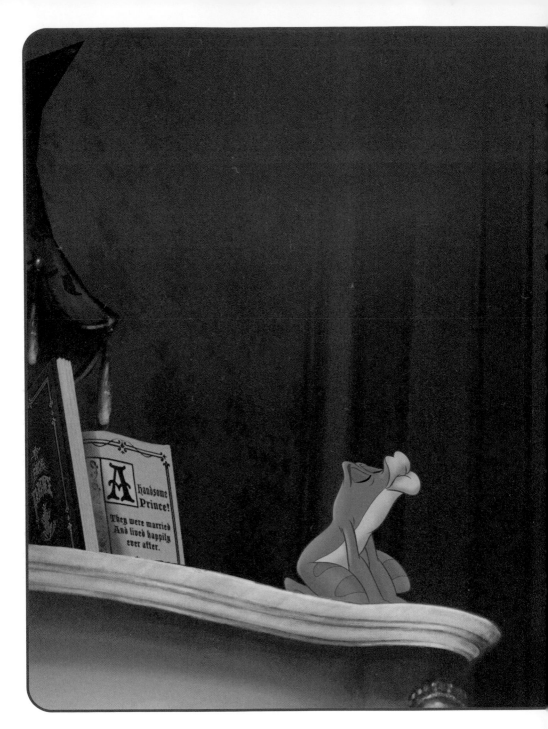

A Handsome
Prince!

They were married
And lived happily
ever after.

The **frog** asked for a kiss.

Tiana gave it a **shot**.

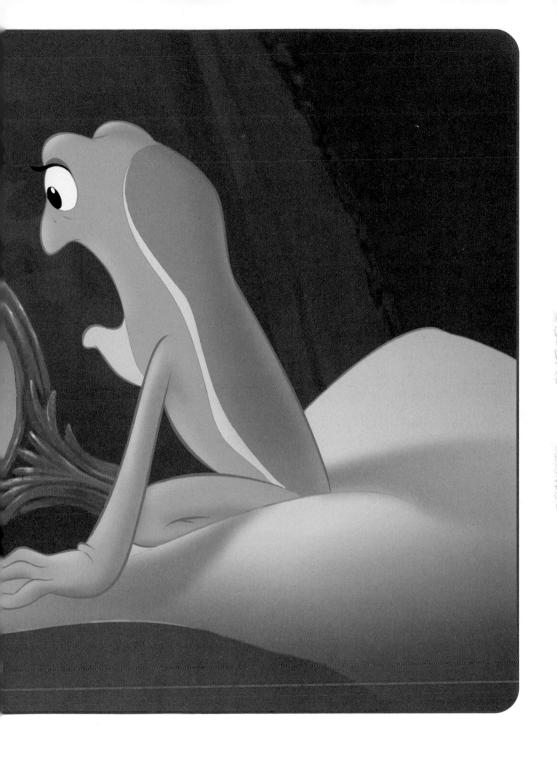

Then Tiana was a **frog**, too!

A **dog** chased the **frogs**.

They **got** away.

But then they were **lost**.

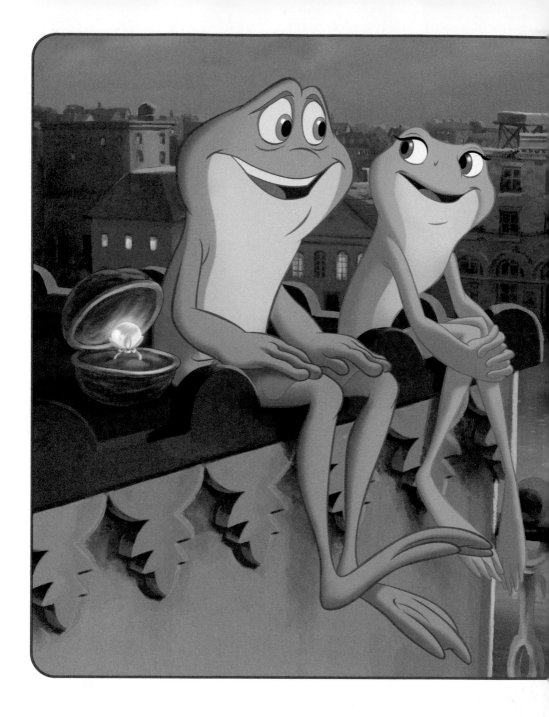

**On** their way home,
they **got along**.

Tiana and Naveen **got** married.
Now they are **not frogs**!

# Tunnel Run

This story is filled with lots of short -u words, which appear in bold type. Here are some to sound out with your child.

| | | |
|---|---|---|
| but | pub | tunnel |
| jump | run | |
| must | shuts | |

Rapunzel and Flynn
are on the **run**.

They find a **pub**.

A man **shuts** the door.

They are trapped!

**But** the **pub** has a **tunnel**.

They **run** through
the **tunnel**.

They **must jump**!

They **jump**!

They made it out
of the **tunnel**.

# Short Vowels Activities

The following pages contain activities to practice comprehension of short vowel sounds. As you go through the activities with your child, encourage them to sound out the words and say their answers out loud.

# Find the Short -a

Cinderella is happy to go to the castle. *Castle* has a **short -a** sound. Point to all the words with the **short -a** sound.

| | |
|---|---|
| tape | mice |
| castle | date |
| happy | sash |
| dress | go |
| mad | sad |

# Find the Rhyme

Cinderella's friends like clothes that match. Rhyming pairs are words with matching sounds at the end. Read the **short -a** words out loud. Use your finger to trace a line between the words that rhyme.

| | |
|---|---|
| can | mad |
| sash | hat |
| sad | fan |
| cat | dash |

# Find the Short -e

Belle's friends are under a spell. *Friends* and *spell* are words that have the **short -e** sound. Point to each word below that has the **short -e** sound.

| best | away | mess | yet |
|------|------|------|------|
| cut | went | tend | jump |
| get | out | for | rest |
| set | under | table | guest |

# Word Families

Belle's new friends treat her like family. Words with the same ending are in the same word family. Can you think of two new words for each word family below? Say them out loud. The first one is done for you!

| met | _s_ et | _l_ et |
| spell | __ell | __ell |
| rest | __est | __est |
| went | __ent | __ent |
| bed | __ed | __ed |

# Short -i Sentences

When the ship tips, Ariel saves the prince. *Ship*, *tips*, and *prince* are all **short -i** words. Come up with your own rescue story using the words below. Try to use at least one **short -i** word in every sentence.

kid

swims

big

fish

sing

win

# Word Escape

Help Ariel escape by pointing to all the words that do <u>not</u> have the **short -i** sound.

| dime | fish | wish |
|------|------|------|
| sad | hide | fin |
| big | chase | swim |
| dish | time | ride |
| ship | flip | mind |

# Short -o Animals

Tiana and Naveen meet lots of animals on their journey. Point to the pictures of animals that are also **short -o** words.

# Find the Rhyme

Tiana is ready to hop home! Read the **short -o** words out loud. Use your finger to trace a line between the words that rhyme.

| | |
|---|---|
| stop | cost |
| lost | bog |
| got | hot |
| frog | hop |

# Find the Short -u

Rapunzel and Flynn are on the run! Point to the words that have the **short -u** sound.

| | |
|---|---|
| jump | trap |
| run | tunnel |
| find | must |
| door | man |
| pub | lot |

# Word Escape

Rapunzel and Flynn must get away. Help them by pointing to all the words that do <u>not</u> have a **short -u** sound.

| | | |
|---|---|---|
| cute | bug | sun |
| view | fun | rat |
| tunnel | beauty | tug |
| fast | drum | tan |
| bit | ran | mud |

# Find Short Vowel Words

Can you point to all the short vowel words in the boxes below?

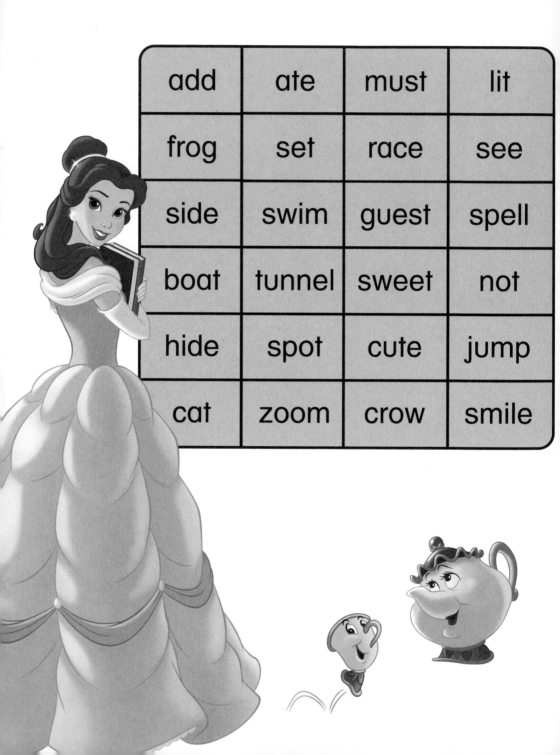

| add | ate | must | lit |
|-----|------|-------|-------|
| frog | set | race | see |
| side | swim | guest | spell |
| boat | tunnel | sweet | not |
| hide | spot | cute | jump |
| cat | zoom | crow | smile |

# Short Vowel Sort

Use your finger to draw a line between words with the same short vowel sound.

get     jump
frog    tend
sad     got
run     sash
ship    fish

# You Did It!

Now you know your short vowel sounds. Read these stories again and again for even more royal phonics fun! You'll be reading like a princess in no time!